THE ROCK N ROLL SINGERS

JERMAINE MORTON

The Rock n Roll Singers

Copyright © 2023 by Jermaine Morton

Paperback ISBN: 978-1-63812-305-7
Ebook ISBN: 978-1-63812-304-0

All rights reserved. No part in this book may be produced and transmitted in any form or by any means, electronic, or mechanical, including photocopying, recording, or by any information storage and retrieval system, without permission in writing from the copyright owner.

The views expressed in this work are solely those of the author and do not necessarily reflect the views of the publisher hereby disclaims any responsibility for them.

Published by Pen Culture Solutions 02/08/2023

Pen Culture Solutions
1-888-727-7204 (USA)
1-800-950-458 (Australia)
support@penculturesolutions.com

THE ROCK N ROLL SINGERS

The setting is in Tucson, Arizona, July 1 1967. a rock n roll band called The Cromatics are touring the western countryside. There gig for July is to perform at an all-girls ranch in Tucson. This is a resort where young females come from around the country to get away and relax in comfort. There's plenty of music and dancing for their entertainment. There's also good food and activities for their enjoyment. The Cromatics roll into Tucson on a tour bus. Greyhound tours! The group does some practicing by doing a little number they made 2 years ago at a teen arts festival from their hometown Newark, NJ. The Comatics grew up in Newark. a band of 7 members who met in junior high and decided to get together as a band? The leader of the group is, Sly Simmons. The band is actually named after him, Sly and The Cromatics. They picked Sly's name because he founded the group 5years earlier, and they like the group Sly and the family Stone so they thought the name would be perfect. Sly's brother, Clyde Simmons is a member of the group. He plays the sax and the bass fiddle. Sly also plays the sax. They have a guy in their group who has a very deep baritone voice for his age. it was unique. So unique he could hit a high note with no problem. He was good at imitating people. his golden voice sounded like Elvis Presley. his idol! He even looks like him. People call him the black Elvis. When, sly heard him sing he was taken away by his golden voice. So much he decided to let him be the lead singer. This young man was, James Deke Rivers. He goes by his middle name Deke. He's also the lead guitarist. His best friend Joseph Hill, better known as Joe, is a member of the group. He's the bands' back up drummer and bongo player. He also plays back up guitarist to Deke. Joe and Deke go back to nursery school on the north side of Newark where they grew up.

The group's lead drummer is Benjamin Jones. Better known as Ben. Certain songs they made using bongos instead of the drums is where Joe fills in. Ben doesn't like the bongos so Joe plays the bongos. Ben grew up on the west side of Newark. So did Sly and Clyde. The band recruited Gregory Morris. who plays bass guitar and back up on the piano. Greg is Native American, from the south side of Newark. He has a dark brown complexion and straight hair. The last member of the group is Mike Rolley. The band's lead pianist.

Mike grew up on the east side of Newark. Everyone got together and formed Sly and the Cromatics. The group has played at many functions, but this was their biggest one. And also the farthest away from home. not to mention their highest paid gig they have done. They didn't get paid for all their gigs they've performed at. Only a good 60% they received money for performing. Each member would receive $200 a week for the time they have spent in Tucson. Their schedule is to be in Tucson for 5 weeks. After their little jam session, Deke takes a look at their schedule and runs through their list of activities.

"Man, this is going to be a lot of fun. Here we are in a lovely vacation resort surrounded by beautiful women. now I ask you what could be better than that?" Deke, asks.

"Look at you, already scheming." Ben says.

"No, I'm not! I'm just looking forward to what's about to happen." Deke replies.

"See, you are going to spend most of your time chasing the girls than you will on your music." Clyde says.

"I can balance the two."

"We heard that before." Sly, says.

"Look I'm not gonna go chasing every girl in sight. I don't do that."

"Oh c'mon! You don't give a female a chance to speak or breathe." Clyde says.

"You be all over them before anybody else gets a chance with them." Greg replies.

"Oh now, Greg I know you're not talking?"

"Hey, I'm not as bad as you."

"Yeah, right! I remember a certain female from Prince Street who you snatched up in less than 10 minutes, just to keep the rest of us from trying to talk to her."

"Oh, but then there's this girl from Dayton, who you took in 30 seconds, just to keep us from saying hello."

"Hey, she liked me."

"So, you say."

"I can't help it if she didn't like yall."

"You didn't give her a chance."

"So, what you saying is, I was blocking yall from getting the girls?"

"Oh no, you haven't blocked anything from me."

"Defensive, are we?"

"No, I'm just letting you know, don't get too sure of yourself."

"Yeah, you're not the only one who can get a girl." Joe says.

"Oh, yes, I know that. I'm no competition compared to you." Deke replies.

"Me?" Joe asks.

"Well- yeah! I can remember a certain young female and her sister that were totally nuts over you."

"He means, Dee Dee and Marisa." Greg says.

"You had those girls falling all over you. they couldn't stop screaming over you. I tell you, Frank Sinatra ain't got nothing on you." Deke, says.

"Don't patronize me, Deke." Joe replies.

"Ah, guys we're here." Clyde says as their bus pulls up into the private roadway of the ranch.

"See, there is a lot of sand out there." Ben says.

"What do you expect to see in the desert?" Sly, asks.

"Hey guys, look over there." Clyde says.

A group of girls gather outside the lounging area of the resort waiting for the bus to arrive.

"Looks as though they are waiting for something." Clyde says.

"Could it be they are waiting for us?" Ben asks.

"Sure, they are. It's no secret that we were coming here." Deke replies.

"We are here to entertain them," Greg, says.

"They do look fine." Clyde replies.

"Hmm! they are so fine." Joe says.

"Fellas, remember why we're here." Sly replies.

"Oh, we remember. Heh heh heh, we're looking at them." Deke, says.

"Deke, you know what I mean." Sly replies.as the bus pulls up to the lobby of the ranch, the girls move closer to the bus to get a look at whose getting off.

"Hey ladies, I think that's them." Sondra says.

"Well, it's about time they got here." Talisa replies.

"I can't wait to see those cute guys." Jill says.

"Jill, can't you control your hormones for at least 5 minutes?" Sondra asks.

"No baby, I can't!" Jill replies.

"Well- heh, heh, heh, you need to calm down." Sondra says.

"You calm down, I'm about to have some fun." Jill replies.

"Now, Sondra, don't act like you don't want any of those guys." Pat, says.

"I'm not gonna drool all over them." Sondra replies.

"But you do want to meet them?" Pat, asks.

"I'm not gonna run around here with my tongue hanging out over no man." Sondra replies.

"You, see how she avoids the question?" Pat, asks.

"I'm not avoiding you- I - just- don't- want to answer you."

"Yeah, sure Sondra."

"Okay, okay, look, I would love to meet them."

"Alright!"

"But! that's as far as it will go."

"Oh, you saying you are not gonna talk to any one of them?"

"No, I'm not saying that."

"So, you will go after one of them?"

"Oh no darling, let me tell you, I will get him to come after me."

"Oh really?"

"Yes, really!"

"So, you want the guy to pursue you?" Susan asks.

"Yes! that's the way it's supposed to be. the man courts the woman."

"Hmm, and you want to give him a hard time?" Pat, asks.

"I didn't say that." Sondra replies.

"So, you plan to use him?" Pat, asks.

"Hmm, not necessarily. I'm just gonna flirt with him. play with him a little bit."

"That doesn't sound right." Susan says.

"Don't worry, I'll be gentle. I'll have the guy eating out of my hand."

"We'll see, Sondra." Pat, says.

The girls stand a few yards away from the bus as the group unloads and vacate the bus. Deke, is the first to get off the bus and the ladies swoon over him. Two girls take a special interest in him. Susan and Connie Jessup. Two sisters who like to die, when they saw, Deke! Jill almost had a heart attack when she saw, Deke. Sly, steps off the bus and girls swoon over him as well. Two sisters, Sonja and Sue Forbes take a big interest into Sly. So does Jill! Clyde steps off the bus and the girls swoon over him with Jill acting a fool. Ben steps off the bus and the girls swoon over him. Greg, steps off the bus and the girls just stop. They smile at him, and then they lose it. Joe, steps off the bus and the girls just died. They couldn't believe how cute he was. As the group walks in, the girls converse over who they liked the best! Connie and Susan loved, Deke as Sonja and Sue loved, Sly. Sondra had her eyes on, Clyde. Now her thing was to get, Clyde interested in her without him knowing that's what she was trying to do. A young lady by the name of Careta Wright sets her sights on, Joe. The group settles in their rooms by the keeper named Mr. MacDonald. MacDonald is overwhelmed that he has celebrities performing at his ranch. even though the Cromatics are far from famous. But they are well known in their hometown. The group settles in their rooms to prepare for their first performance at the theatre that night. The group noticed the girls were swooning over them. They figured after tonight's performance; they would have the girls eating out of their hands. Little did they know that some of the girls were scheming to get a hold of them. Little did the girls know that the group was scheming to get with them also. The group gets everything set on stage for their performance as the girls gather in the theatre to hear them sing. Everything is all set backstage with The Cromatics so the MC goes on stage to announce them. The girls give a round of applause as The Cromatics take the stage and sing the song, 'Wear My Ring Around Your Neck.' The group got a standing ovation for a stunning performance.

"They are hot." Susan says.

"Yes, they are, and they are so fine." Connie replies. "Especially the lead singer."

"Yes, he is a dreamboat."

"I know you would like to meet him."

"I would like to meet them all. But I want to meet him the most."

"Well, you do know where they sleep at."

"Connie, I know what you are thinking."

"And?"

"And we can't do that."

"Why not?"

"They have rules here."

"Girl, rules are made to be broken. besides no one will ever know."

"I don't know."

"C'mon dear sister. You do want to meet this guy, don't you?

"Yes!"

"Okay! Tonight, we'll sneak over to their bungalow so we can meet him."

"That seems risky."

"Sister dear, life is full of risks. c'mon it'll be fun. I promise, nothing will go wrong, okay?"

"Okay!"

The group get together and sing another song titled 'King Creole!' the group receives another standing ovation, for a wonderful performance. The group walks off the stage feeling 10 feet tall as they just brought the house down on their first night in Tucson, Arizona. the MC congratulates The Cromatics on a job well done. the group soon retire to their rooms and prepare for bed. They have a big day tomorrow, so they want a fresh start. meanwhile, Connie and Susan get ready to pay The Cromatics a visit.

"Okay, Susan, let's go."

"Connie, wait, I'm not having a good feeling about this."

"Relax little sister. everything will be alright."

"We could get into trouble."

"Only if we get caught."

"That's what I'm afraid of."

"Don't be! We'll sneak in have a little chat with the guy and then we leave."

"You got it all figured out."

"Absolutely, c'mon let's go."

Connie and Susan sneak over to the barracks where The Cromatics are staying. meanwhile Deke and Joe are still awake. So, Deke, decides to go out for a while.

"Dam my throat is dry. I'm gonna get me a bottle of pop, you want one?"

"No, I'm cool."

"Alright, I'll see you."

Deke steps out and walks around the corner. Meanwhile, Connie and Susan, are down the hall around the other corner coming up in, Deke's direction.

"Which one is his room?" Susan asks.

"Heck if I know, I just came over here with you."

"Well, I thought you knew or had some idea where he was staying."

"I said he was staying over here, didn't I?"

"Yeah!"

"Okay, that narrows it down."

"Good point!"

In about 30 seconds, Deke; will be coming around the corner.

"Do you think his room is on this side?"

"I don't know, Susan, but I'll bet it's on the other side."

"So, let's go check-" Susan, stops in mid-sentence.

"Susan, what's ------wrong?"

The girls are shocked as they see Deke coming down the hall. and, Deke, smiles as he sees' the girls down the hall.

"He------he------hello! How are you?" Susan asks.

"I'm fine and how are you, ladies?

"Oh, we're fine------real fine------aren't we, Susan?"

"Huh? ------oh-------yeah, we fine------we are------f------fine."

"I'm glad to hear that."

"What's your name?" Connie asks.

"My name is, James Deke Rivers. but everyone calls me, Deke."

"Deke! How cool! you have a real cool name."

"Thank you----and who might you be?"

"I'm, Connie, Connie Jessup."

"Nice to meet you, Connie. Deke, says taking Connie, by the hand and giving her a passionate kiss on her hand. "And you are------Susan?"

"Yes------Susan Jessup." Susan, says blushing as Deke, takes her hand and gives her a kiss as well.

"Connie and Susan, such pretty names for two pretty girls."

"Thank you!" Connie and Susan reply. "You know Deke is a fine name for a fine-looking guy."

"Thank you, Connie. my mother gave me that name. She thought it would take me places."

"Hmm, it's doing alright so far."

"Forgive me for asking but--------are you supposed to be in here?"

"No----- not really." Susan replies.

"So------why are you?"

"We had to meet you." Connie replies.

"You had to meet me?"

"Yes! We loved your performance and we just--------hmm-----loved the way you gyrated on stage. we couldn't wait to meet you." Connie replies.

"I'm flattered you like me."

"Yes, we do." Susan replies.

"Uh------we would like to meet the rest of the group too."

"But it's you we had to meet first."

"I'm glad you enjoyed my performance."

"Oh yeah-----you handled that guitar so well; you look so sexy on stage when you play or when you stop playing the guitar." Connie says.

"You mean when I was slapping the guitar?"

"Yeah, that! Oh, you look so cool doing that, I totally freaked out."

"Yeah, I was on the edge of my seat." Susan says.

" You are very sexy Deke, but I guess a lot of girls tell you that?"

"A few do! But I do enjoy the compliment. I am flattered you two ladies find me attractive and my performance so appealing."

"Ooh------he's so polite!" Connie replies.

"He's very gallant."

"And suave."

"Sophisticated!"

"Smooth!"

"Debonair!"

"Okay, ladies, calm down."

"And he's modest." Connie replies.

"And have you noticed how big he is?"

"Yes! Masculinity is very sexy in the right way."

"Hmm, yes, it is, uh Deke how tall are you?"

"I'm 6' 0" tall."

"Oh------God that's up there. We're only 5' 4"."

"You both look lovely."

"Thank you, Deke." They reply. "How much do you weigh?"

"210lbs Susan."

"Dam! And you're not fat? "Connie asks.

"No, I work out every day."

"You're an athlete too?" Susan asks.

"Yes, I am!"

"Oh------God------I'm gonna die, you are so amazing. You can sing play the guitar and you are in good physical shape. Can you dance? I know you can swivel your hips and move around?" Susan asks.

"Yes------I can!"

"Awesome dude! You are incredible."

"I'll bet you are a pretty good lover too?" Connie asks.

"Well------let's just say I don't get too many complaints."

"Ooo------he's so modest. I'll bet you're not the one to kiss and tell?"

"No, Connie I'm not. I believe whatever I do with a girl is between me and her. Out of respect for her and myself, I don't go around talking about what we have or have not done."

"You're very charismatic." Susan says.

"What brought you out here in the hallway?"

"I was gonna get a bottle of pop."

"Oh------Oh------we should be getting back, Connie."

"Yeah! You're right! Well, it was a pleasure meeting you, Deke."

"Oh, the pleasure is all mine."

"We'll see you tomorrow?" Connie asks.

"Yes! tomorrow you get to meet the rest of the group."

"We're looking forward to it" Susan, says. "Bye!"

"Goodbye, Deke!"

"Goodnight, ladies!"

The girls dash back to their room only to run into, Mr. MacDonald on the way.

"Ladies!"

"Mr. MacDonald!" Susan says. "Fancy meeting you here."

"What are you two doing here?"

"Doing here? Us?" Connie asks.

"Yes------you!"

"Well, you see we were------" Susan says.

"We were looking for------a watch."

"We were?" Susan asks.

"Yes!" Connie replies, hitting Susan's arm. "We were looking for, Susan's watch. she dropped it here this earlier."

"And you waited till 11:35 tonight to look for it?"

"Well------you see our mother gave, Susan that watch. for her 13th birthday. It has sentimental value to it. I mean she's had it so long she can't sleep without it."

"And it takes two of yall to look for it?"

"Hey------two heads are better than one."

"Did you find it?'

"No sir we didn't." Susan replies.

"So how are you gonna sleep tonight?"

"Very carefully!"

"Hmm------maybe I should help you look for it."

"Oh no! it's------it's gone, we looked everywhere."

"Well don't give up, Connie. I'm sure we can find it."

"Well sir, we are kinda tired."

"We are?" Susan, asks as she looks at, Connie, who looks at her with the look of befuddlement as, Susan realizes she is supposed to go along with the program. "Oh, yes, we are! We are very, very tired. I am so, so tired, that I yawn, can't hardly keep my eyes open. as you can see, I'm yawning, so that should let you know how tired, I am, ----we----we are. How tired we are." Susan says as, Connie looks at her with the look of now you are over doing it.

"We'll just try again tomorrow."

"Okay, goodnight, ladies."

"Goodnight, Mr. MacDonald." they reply as they haul ass out the barracks and back to their own.

Mr. MacDonald walks away shaking his head. Meanwhile, Deke returns to his room where, Joe is waiting up for him.

"Dam, Deke, did you go to, Jersey for the pop?"

"No but you will never guess who I ran into?"

"Who?"

"I met two young ladies who loved our performance. they're sisters, Connie, and Susan Jessup. they stay in the barracks right across from us."

"They came over here?"

"Yeah, to see us. Well actually they came to see me, but they would like to meet yall too."

"Oh, they would?"

"They look really good. they're both light skin, one has curly brown hair. Which comes over her right eye. the other one has dark brown hair, which is all over her head."

"Hey, I remember seeing some girls that fit that description when we got off the bus today."

"Yeah, they were there."

"So, you interested in one of them?"

"Hell, yeah I'm interested in both of them."

"Hmm two sisters, you've done worse."

"Although I do like one in particular."

"And that is?"

"Susan!"

"Susan?"

"Yes! She was quieter than her sister. She seems a little shy."

"Oh, and I know how you like shy girls."

"Yeah, she was very nice and polite."

"And Connie?"

"She's very nice too and she's more vocal. More outspoken, more daring. You see they're not supposed to be over here this time of night. So, you can say they snuck over here."

"Really they're not allowed over here at all."

"True! But that rule can be bent during day light hours."

"So will we meet these friends of yours?"

"Oh yeah! Tomorrow or later on today."

"Well, I don't know about you, but I'm going to turn in."

"I'm right with you."

Deke and Joe retire to bed while across the way, Connie and Susan couldn't wait to tell the other girls what they did.

"Girls, girls, wake up." Connie says.

"W-what------what's wrong?' Sondra asks.

"Guess what we did?" Connie asks.

"I'm not guessing anything at 1:00 in the morning." Sondra replies.

"We snuck over to the barracks where those rock-n-roll singers are staying." Connie says.

"And we met the lead singer." Susan replies.

"Ooo-----who is he?" Sue, asks.

"His name is Deke Rivers." Connie replies.

"Uh, it's James Deke Rivers. But we can call him Deke."

"Okay, get technical. But the man is an absolute dream."

"Yes, he is so fine, so cool so courteous, so polite."

"I'm happy for yall, now can we go back to sleep?" Sondra asks.

"We'll get to meet the rest of them tomorrow." Susan says.

"Good now if yall excuse me, I'm going back to sleep, goodnight!"

"Goodnight!" everyone say.

The next day, the group is up and taking a tour around the ranch.

"Man, this is great." Clyde says.

"Oh yeah I never seen so much sand and tumbleweeds in my life."

"Mike, you gotta keep an open mind." Clyde says.

"I am but sands not my thang."

"But what about the resort?' Ben asks.

"Oh, the resort is cool. I kinda like it."

"Kinda!" Ben says.

"Yeah, kinda!"

"Well, what's wrong with the resort?" Ben asks.

"Nothing's wrong with the resort itself, it's just surrounded by a lot of sand and desert."

"There's no pleasing you."

"Fellas, there is a whole lot of lovely young ladies out here. Why are we still inside?" Clyde asks.

"We're about to go out now." Ben says.

"I see a flock of girls over at the lounge." Greg says.

"Well, that's where we shall go." Ben replies.

The group stroll over to the lounge to meet the harem of girls who just happen to be Connie and Susan's friends. The guys introduce themselves and the girls do the same. Susan and Connie have already been introduced as sisters and so have Sonja and Sue. Pat Morgan, has been introduced and so has Careta Wright. Vivian Rodriguez and Maria Rodriguez, two cousins from Puerto Rico were introduced. Courtney Phipps and Talisa Roanne were introduced and so was Diane Carter. Jill Conway, the flirtatious one in the group was introduced and last but not least Sondra Clark. The girl who has her eyes set on Clyde. The group found out that the girls are from New Jersey as well. So the guys and girls talk. They get to know a little about one another. The girls are fascinated over

The Cromatics touring the country for the summer. At the same time the guys take interest in certain females. Sly, has his eyes for Sonja and the feelings mutual. Joe has eyes for Careta and those feelings are mutual. We know of Deke and Susan, Clyde and Sondra. Mike has his eyes for Pat, who return the feeling. Ben has eyes for Dianne, whose head over heels for Ben. Greg has his sights for Vivian, whose battling Maria, for him. Not to mention Talisa, has her eyes for Joe and Courtney, has her eyes for Ben. Sue, have eyes for Sly and Connie have eyes for Deke and Jill has eyes for everybody. The girls mention a dance that's going on that night at the town hall. Now The Cromatics were not performing that night. nor were they invited to the party, But the group gets the idea to crash the party. And that's exactly what they do. The Cromatics walk in the townhall casually, looking around the place. They see a lot of girls there, but they don't see any of the girls they met earlier. They walk over to the table to get a drink. Then they separate to see if they can find some action. Meanwhile, Sondra peeps out The Cromatics and walks over to them, before they could split up.

"Well, I don't see anyone we know in here so I'm gonna take a look around." Deke, says.

"Yeah, maybe you'll get lucky." Joe says.

"Well, well, well, what are you guys doing here?" Sondra asks.

"We came to join the party." Sly replies.

"Well, the last I heard, you have to be invited to join a party." Sondra says.

"Look, we are the entertainment around here." Sly replies.

"Not tonight you're not." Sondra says.

"What's the big deal, we came to your party?" Deke, asks.

"Yeah, obviously we wanted to see yall again, so we came to------" Ben, says.

"------crash the party. yeah, yeah, I understand. But we have rules around here. You don't go where you're not invited. Now I suggest you guys hightail it out of here before you get caught, chow." Sondra says walking away.

"Man is she hospitable." Clyde replies.

"None the less, I'm not leaving." Deke, says.

"Hey, Mike and Joe have found Talisa, maria and Vivian." Greg replies.

"Well, that's what I'm gonna do." Deke, says.

"What, talk to Talisa, Maria and Vivian?" Greg asks.

"No, I'm gonna talk to the other girls." deke replies.

"We could get into trouble." Ben says.

"Ah, I was born in trouble." Deke, replies.

"You know they could have the same attitude as, Sondra." Clyde says.

"Well, we'll find out, won't we?" Deke replies.

"Yeah, why don't you show us how it's done, Deke."

"Oh, Sly you want me to do your talking for you?"

"Oh no don't get it wrong. I will do my own talking. We just want to see how easy it is for you to do it."

"Suit yourself! I'll start with Sonja and Sue."

"Hey, Sonja is off limits to you"

"Relax, I'm just gonna talk to her that's all."

Deke walks over to where Sonja and Sue are and strikes up a conversation.

"Is anybody sitting here?" Deke, asks.

"No!" Sonja replies.

"Do you ladies mind if I join you?" Deke, asks.

"No!" Sonja replies.

Deke sits down in a seat between Sue and Sonja. he leans back crosses his left leg over his right and strikes up a conversation.

"So, how are you ladies?"

"We are fine!" Sue, says.

"Now you guys know this is a private party." Sonja says.

"We know, but we had to see what the action was here."

"What do you mean by action?" Sonja asks.

"What I meant was we wanted to see what a party in Tucson was like."

"I don't believe you." Sonja says.

"It's true!"

"I don't believe what you say."

"Okay, what do you think we came in here for?"

"I think you came in here to meet girls."

"So do I."

"Hmm, you girls are very perceptive. Well, the truth is we did come here to meet girls."

"That's what we thought." Sonja says.

"But I'll bet you didn't think it was you and your friends we came to see."

"Get out! you came to see us?" Sonja asks.

"Yes! I can tell you that the leader of the group, Mr. Sly Simmons, has a special interest in you, Sonja."

"He does?" Sonja asks with a sheepish smile. "So why didn't he tell me himself?"

"Yeah, what are you, his messenger?"

"No, I'm not. Sly will talk to you."

"And when will that be?"

"He will be over right now." Deke, says standing up and waving over to, Sly to come over.

"Well fellas that's my cue." Sly, says.

"Excuse me girls, I have some business to attend to. I'll see yall later, bye." Deke, says getting up and walking away as Sonja and Sue look astonished. Sly, comes over to their table to talk. Deke walks over to where Jill, Sondra, and Dianne are sitting.

"Hello, Jill." Deke says kissing her. "Hello, Dianne." he says kissing her. "Hello, Sondra!" he says kissing her.

"Hey, you don't know me well enough to be kissing me." Sondra says.

"What are you so offensive for? I didn't kiss you on your lips."

"It doesn't matter you don't put your lips on me."

"Okay, fine! Have it your way. So how are you ladies doing?"

"We're doing well." Dianne replies.

"Yeah, don't worry about her. She's just mad because it's past her bedtime and she's not used to being out late."

"Oh, that's what it is?"

"Yeah, there's really nothing wrong with what you did." jill says.

"Hmm, you didn't mind me kissing you?"

"Oh no I didn't mind. it was just a friendly kiss. I'm sure you didn't mean anything by it."

"Hmm, I'm sure I didn't. Did you mind me kissing you, Dianne?"

"No, I did not."

"Good! Well, I'm glad everything is all right over here. I'll see you girls later. goodbye!" Deke, says walking away. he walks over to where Pat and Connie are sitting. "Hello, Pat!" Deke says kissing her. now before Deke, could walk around the table and greet, Connie, she quickly jumps up and runs into, Deke's arms and kisses him.

"Hello, Connie! How are you?"

"I'm fine!" Connie says kissing him. "Just fine!" She replies kissing him again. "Really, really, fine!" she says kissing him again.

"Okay, okay! Uh------where is your sister?"

"She's over there."

"Where?"

"Over there, c'mon let's go over there." Deke walks over to Susan with Connie on his arm.

"Hello, Susan!"

"Hello, Deke!"

"How are you?"

"Fine!"

"Why are you sitting here by yourself?"

"I'm bored! There's no one here for me to talk too. Well, there are no guys here that I am interested in talking too."

"Well, if you like you can talk to me."

"I'm------ I am a little------"

"Shy? There's no reason to be. I don't bite. I mean you didn't seem to shy last night."

"Oh------about last night------"

"Of course, Connie did most of the talking."

"Well, I was just trying to break the ice."

"And so, you did."

"Deke------I------I want to tell you something."

"What is it Susan?"

"I------that is I------ would like to see more of you if that is okay. I mean if you have time for me, that is, if you're not too busy?"

"Susan, I'd love to spend time with you."

"You would?"

"Yes! In fact, that's why I'm here, to see you."

"You are?" Susan asks.

"You are?" Connie asks.

"Yes, I enjoyed our little meeting last night so I crashed the party so I could see you again."

"You did?" Susan asks.

"You did?" Connie asks.

"Yes, I did."

Soon Vivian comes over to their table and Deke, stands up to greet her.

"Hello, Vivian!"

"Hi, ya doing, Deke?"

"I'm fine, how are you?"

"I'm fine!"

"That's good to hear. So, Susan, are you going on the hayride tomorrow?"

"Yes! we all are, Deke."

"Good! We can spend some more time together then."

"I'd like that."

Sly, gives the signal to Deke, that they must leave. Deke, walks over to Susan and takes her by the hand and starts to caress it very gently.

"I will see you tomorrow."

"Yes, Deke!"

"Okay, you have a pleasant evening." Deke, says as he leans in and kisses Susan, passionately.

"Goodnight, ladies!" Deke says walking across the room.

"Hmm, he is a very charming young man." Vivian says.

"Yeah, and he does have a likeness for Susan."

"Connie!"

'"Well it's true."

"It is girl, I can see that."

"Yeah, I think he does, he said he came here to see me."

"Well girl that proves it. he likes you" Vivian, says.

"Yeah, I guess he does."

The group heads back to their rooms and retire.

CHAPTER 2

The next day the group gets ready to go on the hayride with the girls. Deke and Sly stop by the girl's barracks before they leave.

"Hello, Susan." Deke says kissing her.

"Hi, Deke."

"Hello, Sonja!" Sly says kissing her.

"Hello, Sly,"

"How are you?" Deke, asks.

"I'm fine how are you?" Susan asks.

"Fine!"

"Aren't you guys coming with us?" Sonja asks.

"Yes! That's why we're here." Sly replies.

"That's why what?" Sonja asks.

"We're here!" Deke replies.

"You're here?" Susan asks.

"Yes!" Deke replies.

"Why?" Sonja asks.

"To take yall on the hayride." Sly replies.

"You're taking us?" Sonja asks.

"Yes! I'll be driving the truck and the rest of the group will be on board to entertain you." Sly says.

"OOO, I like that." Sonja says.

"So, yall ready to go?" Sly, asks.

"Yeah, let's go." Sonja replies.

The girls board the truck with The Cromatics and off they go downtown to the flea market on a hayride. On the way Deke, sings a song titled 'Old MacDonald'. After the song, Sly pulls up into the market. The Cromatics are amazed at what they see.

"What's the matter Deke." Susan asks.

"Uh nothing------I'm just surprised that there is a flea market in the desert."

"Well Tucson isn't all desert."

"I see there is a little city going on down here."

"Let me show you around. Now you see those antiques over there?"

"Antiques?"

"Yes------you never been to a flea market before?"

"No------ not really."

"Well, it's a good thing I'm here to show you around."

"Lead on!"

"As I was saying the antiques over there, the kerosene lamps have some value to them."

"Is that why they cost so much."

"Exactly! Now look at the clothes. they have clothes worn back in the 40's, 50's, and early 60's.

and look-----they even have the latest fashion bell bottoms."

"You'll never catch me wearing those."

"Me either. Now they have clothes going back to the 1930's like the zoot suits. I like them."

"Yes, they really did look good on a man."

"OOO------who you telling? My father has one of those suits. I love looking at the pictures he has when he used to wear his suit. And my uncle used to have one too. He also used to work at a flea market. I used to work there with him when I was little. The customers couldn't stop buying things from me."

"I guess they couldn't say no to such a pretty little girl."

"Thank you, Deke you say the sweetest things."

"Hey, I only speak the truth."

"Hmm, that you do! Those were the good times."

"You said your uncle used to work at a flea market?"

"Yeah, he died in an automobile accident two years ago. A truck ran into him, trying to pass another vehicle."

"Is that the incident where a man was pinned under a truck for 48 hours?"

"Yes!"

"I'm sorry that happened."

"So am I. I cried every night for a week when I found out what happened. I loved him so much. I couldn't believe he was gone. But I did get pass it. I knew I couldn't bring him back, but I would never forget about him."

"You, okay?"

"Oh, yeah, I'm fine!"

"So, you wanna get some lunch?"

"Sure, let's go!" Susan says kissing Deke.

Meanwhile, Sly and Sonja, are on the other side of the market having lunch.

"Sly, how did you get the group started, The Cromatics?"

"Well, me and the guys met back in junior high. This was 5 years ago. We used to play at school functions all the time. Now when we started, we didn't really get along. But after a while we got used to each other. We practiced a lot after school. and on weekends. After it all clicked in, we started getting some recognition. A record producer heard us play at the school and he liked us. He sent us on tours to different high schools throughout New Jersey. He booked this gig for us here in Tucson. And I must say, me and the group is enjoying every minute of it. Especially now that we made a few friends."

"You mean me and the girls?"

"Yes, I do!"

"OOO------I'm flattered! So when do yall graduate?'

"Next year."

"Uh------huh! And what are yall plans for the future?"

"We plan to record our first album, due to come out in the fall of 68. We're gonna start working on it in the spring of next year. But it won't be completed until the fall like say October. We're also gonna go to college and study performing arts. Music number one, and we each have our own interest to major in college."

"So, you're gonna be college boys and musicians at the same time?"

"Yes! And someday a movie contract could be in the works?"

"Wow! Yall certainly have your life planned out."

"Well------there is room for more ideas."

"I have one question for you."

"What?"

"You're the leader of the group, so why is Deke the lead singer?'

"Because of his voice. He has a unique singing voice. So we all agreed that Deke would be perfect to sing the lead on all our songs. And he does have a way of attracting the audience by swiveling his hips."

"OOO----yes he does. You know he is really sexy when he performs on stage."

"Uh------huh------anyway."

"He has a nice muscular body that is ooo------too good to be true."

"Uh------huh------anyway."

"I mean he looks so cool and so good I say he is irresistible."

"Uh------huh------okay-----I get it."

"Oh------don't get me wrong, Sly, I like, Deke in all but-----I'm interested in you."

"That's good because I am also interested in you." Sly, says kissing, Sonja.

"Why didn't you make Deke the leader of the group?"

"Because he is not responsible for us being together. I am. Besides my name sounds better, Sly and The Cromatics. See listen how that sound, Sly and The Cromatics. sounds good, don't it?"

"Yes, it does!"

"We better head back to the truck."

"Oh------is it that time already?"

"Yes, it is!"

"Well, let's go!"

Meanwhile, back with Susan and Deke.

"Susan, I must tell you that this is the most fun I ever had with any girl I ever been with in my life."

"I'm glad! Because I never had so much fun with any other boy like I have with you."

"I'm glad to hear that." Deke says kissing Susan. "We better head back to the truck."

"Okay!"

Susan and Deke head back and meet up with Sly and Sonja. Careta and Sondra are on their way back as well and they have a little disagreement about Sondra's, methods on getting, Clyde to talk to her. The rest of the group and the girls join everyone and they are ready to go. On the way back Deke, sings 'Old MacDonald' for a second time. As everyone get back to the ranch the group say goodbye to the girls and head to the theatre to rehearse for their gig the next day. It's the 4th of July and everyone is in the mood of free spirit and independence. Everyone gathers in the theatre to hear The Cromatics sing. Now the song The Cromatics are gonna sing requires a dance by a young lady in the number. Deke, asks Careta, if she would dance on stage with The Cromatics. She accepts and she was a hit along with the Cromatics. The Cromatics sing 'Hey Little Girl'. A song, Deke came up with from watching an old Elvis movie. Everyone applaud for Sly and The Cromatics plus Careta. Backstage, Sly congratulates Careta, on a job well done.

And so does Deke, who congratulates himself on a job well done as well. Now the group packs up their instruments and get ready to move to the fairgrounds where a festival is going on that night for the 4th of July. The guys meet up with the girls at the festival, and Sondra finally has her talk with Clyde.

"Clyde!"

"Sondra!"

"How are you?"

"Fine!"

"Good!"

"And yourself?"

"Oh, I'm fine. fine as can be."

"Hmm------yes you are."

"Okay, I'm gonna get right down to it, Clyde------I------I-----I like you."

"You like me?"

"Yes, I like you a lot. And I want to get to know you better."

"You do?"

"Yes, I like the way you play the bass."

"You do?"

"Yes!"

"I'm glad because I love to dazzle people with my music. The bass is my favorite instrument. When I was 10 years old my father bought me a bass for my birthday. I played that thing every night and day. That's how I got to be so good now. I love listening to songs that use the bass. Actually, it's called the bass fiddle. But I love it none the less."

"You listen to the songs from the 50's."

"Oh yeah! My favorite song is 'all shook up' by Elvis, recorded back in 1957. It was good. I love the bass in that song. 1957 was the year for a lot of songs using the bass fiddle. Ever heard 'A Whole Lotta Shaking Going On' by Jerry Lee Lewis?"

"Yes!"

"That was a good song. wonderful bass! That was all I did back in the 50's listen to music and play music."

"Gee, the only thing I was doing in 57 was playing with may dolls."

"You play with dolls?"

"Yes! I'm a girl. Girls play with dolls."

"Well, you don't look like------"

"I'm older now that's why. I'm 18 years old. I don't play with dolls. But I did 10 years ago."

"OOO------very touchy. Okay, you used to play with dolls. Just like I used to play with balloons, I slept with a teddy bear, I used to make train tracks in my oatmeal."

"Wait a minute, you use to sleep with a teddy bear?"

"Yes!"

"I can't picture you sleeping with a teddy bear."

"Well, I'm older now. I'm 17 years old. I don't sleep with teddy bears. But I did 10 years ago."

"Heh, heh, heh, touché!"

"You know Sondra, I like you too. I would like to get to know you better also."

"You do?"

"Yes, I do!"

Now Sondra, relaxes as Clyde, takes over the pursuit and shows a lot of attention and affection for Sondra.

Meanwhile Susan and Deke run off to a secluded spot away from the others.

"Susan, did I ever tell you how pretty you are?"

"Yes! The first time we met."

"And did I tell you that I like you very much?'

"Yes------the third time we met."

"You know we only have a few weeks to be together."

"I know, that's not enough time."

"But we will be separated for a very long time when we leave."

"I know that's why we shouldn't worry about that. We should just enjoy the time we have now.
And let tomorrow take care of tomorrow."

"I agree with you." Deke says kissing Susan. Soon Connie comes over to where Susan and Deke are at."

"How are you two?"

"We're cool. So, what brings you here and how did you find us?"

"I just followed the smell of love in the air. Besides the festival is a little dull. We need something to liven it up."

"Too bad we don't have a piano I could play a tune for you."

"You play the piano?" Connie asks.

"Yes, I can also play the drums."

"Hey, I want to hear you play the piano."

"I don't have a piano with me Susan."

"Yeah, but the theatre does." Connie, says.

"Excuse me?"

"The theatre. The Cromactics have spare keys to get in don't yall?" Connie asks.

"Yeah!"

"So------we'll go there tonight and listen to you play the 88 keys for us."

"Only you could come up with these ideas for breaking into places after hours."

"But it's not breaking in if you have the keys."

"Let's go Deke!" Susan says.

"Yeah, let's go."

"Okay girls!"

The trio heads for the theatre and come in through the back door.

"It's dark in here."

"That's because the lights are out, Susan." Deke says disappearing in the dark.

"Are you afraid of the dark Susan?"

"No, I'm not, Connie. I'm just saying its dark in here."

"Well, you never been here in the dark, before."

"Neither have you."

"Well, I'm not afraid."

"I'm not afraid either."

"Okay you're not afraid Susan I'm sorry I said you were."

"Don't patronize me, Connie."

"I'm not patronizing you, Susan."

`

"Yes, you are."

"Okay I apologize if I sounded like I was patronizing you, Susan."

"You're doing it again, Connie."

"No, I'm not."

"Yes, you are."

"Look you'll feel better when the lights come on."

"Yeah, hey, Deke did you find the lights yet?"

Connie and Susan listen to pure silence as Deke, doesn't respond.

"Deke, did you find the lights?"

Connie and Susan listen to pure silence again.

"Deke! Deke! Deke stop playing. Deke! Deke where are you?"

Deke slowly sneaks up behind Susan.

"Deke------Deke------where are you?"

Deke reaches out to touch Susan on her shoulder.

"Deke!"

"What?"

"Ouch! Suzan screams as she nearly has a heart attack as Deke touches her shoulder. "You scared the life out of me boy."

"I'm sorry, I couldn't resist."

"Oh, you couldn't?"

"No, I couldn't." Deke says turning on the lights.

"You almost scared me to death. I am very upset with you Deke."

"I'm sorry I scared you, Susan. I promise I won't scare you again, okay?"

"Don't you patronize me, Deke."

"Oh------God!" Connie says. "He's not patronizing you, Susan."

"I'm not patronizing you, Susan."

"Yeah, he's not patronizing you, Susan."

"Yes, he is, both of you are."

"Sweetheart------come here. Sit down at the piano. I want to play something for you."

Deke, sat down at the piano with Susan, sitting on his left and Connie, on his right. He starts to play a tune for them. An old song he wrote 6 years ago titled "Tender Hearts" Susan, gives Deke, a big hug before he could finish the song. She loved the song so much gave Deke, a big kiss. And she did forgive Deke, for scaring her half to death. Deke takes the girls back to their rooms. Deke, tells the girls of one of their routines The Cromatics do when they perform. He explains the art of guitar slapping in their performances. Which is very common in their business among rock n roll musicians.

CHAPTER 3

The next day, everybody's' at the theatre waiting to hear The Cromatics sing. Susan goes backstage to give Deke a kiss for good luck as The Cromatics come on stage. The Cromatics sing "Teddy Bear" a song Elvis, did 10 years earlier. Everyone applauds for Sly and The Cromatics. Susan, greets Deke, with another kiss backstage.

"You were great Deke."

"Thank you, Susan!"

"Hey, what about the rest of us?" Clyde asks.

"Oh, yall were fabulous."

"I'm glad you liked us." Clyde says.

"Yes, your bass playing was wonderful."

"I'm glad you liked it."

Sonja, and Jill come backstage to see The Cromatics.

"Hello, Sly!"

"Hello, Sonja!"

"Might I speak to you privately Mr. Simmons?"

"Yes, you may Miss Forbes."

Sonja and Sly slip out the back door as Susan, say goodbye to, Deke and walk out to the audience with Clyde and Ben as Jill, talk to Deke.

"I enjoyed your performance, Deke."

"Thank you, Jill."

"I gotta tell you I love the way you move your sexy body."

"Thank you, Jill."

"You know what I like to do, Deke?"

"What?"

Jill walks up real close to Deke.

"Do you really want to know what I want to do?" Jill, asks rubbing her hand on Deke's, chest.

"What, Jill?"

"I want to spend some time with you."

"Okay!"

"You don't mind?"

"No, I don't mind."

"I also would like too-----well------you know!"

"No------what?"

"You know!"

"No, I don't"

"Deke, you don't know?"

"No, I don't"

"You really don't know?" Jill, asks kissing, Deke.

"OOO------oh boy."

"Now you know?"

"I think so!"

"You don't mind?"

"No------ I don't mind at all."

"Come on to my room."

"Is it safe?"

"Don't worry! Everything's gonna be alright."

Deke and jill go to her room and spend the next 6 hours alone in each other's arms. When, Deke leaves he runs into, Joe coming out of Careta's, room. Joe and Deke look at each other in surprise then they shake each other's hand and head back to their barracks. The next day Sly, Sonja, Deke, and Susan go for a ride through the mountains. Deke, breaks out in a song titled 'Promise Land', while they drive through the canyons. On their way back they stopped at the flea market.

"Now tell me this doesn't look ridiculous?" Sonja asks.

"It does!" Susan says.

"Yes, that dress is bad." Sly, says.

"Now you see these pants and this shirt it's just awful." Sonja says.

"Where have I seen that style at?" Deke, asks.

"From Jill!" Sonja says.

"Jill!" Deke replies.

"Yes! she wears clothes like this. Man, what a girl."

"You don't like her?" Deke, asks.

"Oh no I love her. I just don't like her taste in clothes. It makes her look too sexy------like a

floozie."

"Too sexy!" Deke, says.

"Like a floozie!" Susan replies.

"Yes! She likes to show off her figure, and her clothes. That's her way of attracting guys, by flirting."

"Oh really!" Deke, says.

"Her clothes are expensive like yours, Deke."

"Like mine?"

"Yes! You wear the expensive levi suits."

"Of different colors." Susan says.

"Exactly!" Sonja replies.

"Oh, come now."

"Listen you've been here 6 days and 5 nights and you've wore 5 different color suits and you criss crossed 2 of them." Sonja says.

"That includes the one you're wearing." Susan replies.

"I like the denim look. Am I too sexy for yall?"

"No, you're not! "Susan says.

"Certainly not!" Sonja replies.

"Come on people, let's head back to the ranch." Sly, says.

Everyone gets back in the car and head back to the ranch.

CHAPTER 4

Later, back at the ranch, a bulletin was posted up to inform everyone that a new band would be coming to the ranch. A group called Pazzaz, that was scheduled to perform after the Cromatics in August. But an error was made in the booking arrangements. Now Pazzaz will be coming in on July 11, and they will be performing with the Cromatics. Now the band isn't too happy to hear that another band is coming to play during their spotlight. but Sly, reassures the group that they have nothing to worry about. They will still get paid as if they were the only group there and they won't lose any publicity. Two days later the group Pazzaz is on their way to Tucson.

"Well fellas, in 3 days we'll be in Tucson." James says.

"I hear there'll be a lot of girls out there." John says.

"Oh yeah, there will be a lot of girls there." James says.

"Hmm, I can't wait to have me some fun with a little cutie." John says.

"Relax, John, the girls could already have boyfriends."

"You think I care about that, James?"

"No!"

"Heh, heh, James doesn't care about that either." Jim says.

"And you know that! I intend to be up in every and any girl that catches my eye. No matter who is around." James replies.

"Shouldn't we keep our mind on business?" Johnny asks.

"This is business. Risky business!" James replies.

"This is gonna be a wonderful trip." Jim says.

"I heard there was another band performing there." John says.

"Impossible! We are the only band to perform at this ranch." James says.

"You sure?" Johnny asks.

"Oh yeah! I booked it myself. I know we are the only ones to be there. Let me tell you, this will boost up our careers. If we are a hit in Tucson, we'll be on the charts for the top 40 instead of the top 100. then we'll go to the top 20, top 10 and then we'll go to number 1. Once we reach number 1; we'll be on top.

We'll be the best jazz band in the country." James replies.

"Well, I'm with it." Jim says.

"I'm telling you guys we are gonna blow any other band off this planet. Pazzaz will be the best this country has ever seen." James says. At 10:00 in the morning on July 11th, the tour bus with Pazzaz on it, pulls into the ranch. The Cromatics and the girls are standing outside waiting for them to step off the bus. The group gets off the bus and are amazed at the lovely young ladies they see.

"Hmm, look what we got here. A welcoming committee. Beautiful girls and look, we even got our own personal bell boys." James says.

"Is he referring to us?" Ben asks.

"I think so." Mike replies.

"So how are you ladies doing?" James asks.

"Fine! Sondra replies.

"That's good! Allow me to introduce us. I'm James Coburn, the leader of the group Pazzaz. and I'm also the lead singer. Now this guy right here is my drummer, Jim Daniels. My man Slim here is my sax man. My guitarist is John Sacks. My pianist is Johnny Tyrone. My bass player is Joey Miller and last but not least is, Johnny Taylor. He's my back up saxophone player. Now I play the guitar and I can also play the sax. I'm a heavy saxophone player. and might I say I am the best there is." James says.

"Conceited, isn't he?" Greg asks.

"Very much!" Deke replies.

The girls introduce themselves to Pazzaz. James turns to The Cromatics for them to pick up his bags.

"Yall are some pretty young ladies. you guys can grab our bags and take them to our rooms."

James says.

"You talking to us?" Sly, asks.

"Yes!" James replies.

"Are you crazy, what do we look like to you?" Sly, asks.

"Bell boys!" James replies.

"Hold up we ain't nobody's bell boy." Sly, says.

"Well, who the hell are you?" James asks.

"We're Sly and The Cromatics. I'm Sly, Sly Simmons."

"I'm, Clyde!"

"I'm, Deke!"

"I'm, Joe!"

"I'm, Ben!"

"I'm, Greg!"

"And I'm, Mike!"

"Sly and The Cromatics? What are yall doing here?" James asks.

"We're performing here." Sly replies.

"Performing? Here? You guys?" James asks.

"Yes!" Sly replies.

"Wait a minute. We are supposed to be here."

"No, no, no! You guys are supposed to be here next month. This month was booked for us."

"No, no, no------you got your facts wrong."

"No, Mr. Coburn you got your facts wrong. Our agent booked us here in Tucson for the month of July. You guys were for the month of august. It's posted in the hall. Mr. MacDonald will tell you. He has all our bookings."

"This can't be. No not another band. No not another band."

"What's wrong with that, James? There's enough people here for both of us to entertain." Ben says.

"No, no, no, I am the main attraction here. My band and me. Pazzaz."

"Well, that's not gonna happen because The Cromatics are here." Sly, says.

"You guys are gonna have to leave. Pazzaz shares the spotlight with no one."

"We aren't going anywhere." Sly replies.

"Look, Sly don't let me tell you twice."

"Hold up, what are you trying to say?" Clyde asks, walking over to James.

"Relax, Clyde! He's not gonna do anything to us."

"Wanna bet?" James asks.

"Well, what are you waiting for?" Clyde asks.

"For you clowns to leave."

"We're not leaving till it's our time to leave."

"Your time is now."

"Says who?"

"Says me, James Coburn, leader of Pazzaz."

"Look, James, stop trying to bully us. We're not leaving and that's that." Sly, says.

"We'll see about that."

"Look guys, yall can work here together. There's really no problem with both groups performing here together." Sondra says.

"Pazzaz performs with no one."

"That's not a good attitude to take James."

"Look! We have a gig to do tonight."

"Perfect! The Cromatics aren't performing tonight, are you?" Sondra asks.

"No!" Sly replies.

"Good! Then yall can alternate. Whenever The Cromatics don't sing Pazzaz will." Sondra says.

"I like that idea." Careta says.

"So do I!" Pat, replies.

"Well, I don't."

"James, you are being selfish." Sondra says.

"So, we get to perform tonight?"

"Yes! you might knock'em dead." Sondra says.

"Might?"

"Okay you will." Sondra says.

"Very, conceited!" Greg replies.

"Hmm! Come along fellas let's get settled in and get ready for work."Pazzaz goes to check in their rooms and get ready for their performance.

"I tell you fellas, I don't see us getting along with those guys." Ben says.

"I don't either." Deke replies.

"I don't like that guy, James." Susan says.

"Yeah, he doesn't soothe me too well either." Clyde replies.

"I think he's kinda sexy." Jill says.

"You think everybody is sexy." Deke replies.

"Well, there are some who are sexier than others." Jill says sliding over to Deke.

"I can imagine." Deke replies.

"Let's see if these clowns can sing better than us." Greg says.

"I know they can't" Clyde, replies.

"Relax fellas! we don't have anything to worry about. We are not in competition with anybody. Besides we have a contract. Nobody's beating us out of that, so relax. Let's go watch the show." Sly, says. That night the group Pazzaz comes out to perform at the theatre. Everyone gave a warm welcome for Pazzaz. The group sings the song 'At the hop!' Which is a remake of the original from 1957. Making it a jazz tune from the original rock n roll tune. Everyone applauds for Pazzaz when they finished their number. Even The Cromatics were impressed by their music. The Cromatics went backstage to congratulate them.

"Hey, James, you guys were terrific."

"Were we? I believe it was------Sly. Sly Simmons. correct?" James asks, sarcastically. "Now you boys didn't have to come back here and tell me and my men how good we are. We know that we are. But it's good you realize; how good we are. As long as you do, we'll get along fine. Come along boys, we must retire." James says as he and Pazzaz exit the theatre.

"Sly, I don't think these guys are gonna be too friendly." Clyde says.

"Nonetheless we are gonna do what we gotta do." Sly replies.

CHAPTER 5

The next day The Cromatics are at the festival ready to sing to their ladies. Deke, grabs a seat next to Susan and Connie and belts out a tune titled 'I got lucky!' After their performance, Deke, rolls over to rap with the rest of The Cromatics. Meanwhile James Coburn slips up to talk to Susan.

"Hello, Susan!"

"Hi, ------James!"

"OOO, do I sense a little tension in your voice?"

"Yes!"

"Why?"

"Because!"

"Because what?"

"because of you!"

"Me? What have I done to you?"

"You haven't done anything to me."

"So why are you mad at me?"

"I don't like your attitude."

"What's wrong with my attitude?"

"Your arrogant, conceded, you think you are the best and nobody can compete with you."

"Well, I am the best and nobody can compete with me."

"See what I mean?"

"Hey, should I be ashamed of my talents?'

"No!"

"Should I not be the best at what I do, whatever I do?"

"Yeah!"

"Okay, so what's the problem?"

"It's no crime at wanting to be the best, James. But it is a crime to rub everybody's nose in it. And then when someone pays you a compliment, you throw it back in there face as if, they need to congratulate you."

"Hey, I am glad they see the talent I am so well blessed with."

"I guess you are."

"And you do too."

"Oh, don't flatter yourself."

"Oh, you already done that for me."

"I did?"

"See you admit it."

"Don't play with me, James."

"I'm not playing, I'm dead serious. You know you like what you see. I know that you know you like what you see. So, it's you who shouldn't play with me."

"You are so full of yourself."

"Look baby I am the best at what I do. No need in denying it. And I know you are impressed by it."

"You wish!"

"Do I? Look I can see it all in your eyes. Your face gives you away."

"Meaning?"

"Meaning, you are fascinated by me my dear."

"Oh please!"

"Yes, you are! I know you can't stand me. But you are fascinated with me. I'm too egotistical!
some might say I'm a pompass. But nonetheless, I peeked your interest. You wanna know how can such a fine young man of my grace, talent, and stamina can be so cruel, shrewd and such a roole of a man."

"Oh, you are so far out there."

"Maybe, but you wanna see what makes me fly out there."

"You're joking?"

"Am I? You want to know so much about me little girl, but you are afraid to ask."

"And why is that?"

"Because you are afraid of what you might find. You see you have a goody goody nature to you. Why I have a bad boy image to me. You are afraid that you might like what you loathe so much."

"Unbelievable!"

"Is it?"

"Well, it was nice talking with you, but I must be going."

"Okay! But before you go let me leave you something to think about."

"And what's that?"

James puts his arm around Susan's, waist and pulls her closer to him. They look into each other's eyes and James, passionately kisses, Susan.

"Till we meet again my sweet." James, kisses, Susan again and leaves.

Two days later, Deke, meets up with Courtney. They spend time together and realize they have a lot in common. They also find out they are attracted to each other. One thing leads to another as they talk and they kiss. They talk and they caress. They caress and kiss and talk. Soon they start to remove each other's clothing until they're both naked. They spend the next 6 hours together before, Deke goes back to his barracks.

CHAPTER 6

On July 17th, Pazzaz is ready to give another exciting performance. The group comes out to perform, 'The bird'. An old 1963 classic. The group receives a round of applause for their performance.

"Looks like they are becoming a hit in Tucson." Clyde says.

"Do you think we lost our audience?" Joe asks.

"No, we couldn't have." Ben replies.

"Why not, it happens to entertainers all the time." Greg says.

"Yeah, you saw what happened to Elvis, when he started making those movies." Clyde replies.

"Yeah, The Beatles came and took over." Ben says.

"And they're still kicking ass." Mike replies.

"But we haven't been out of circulation that long." Greg replies.

"It don't take that long to be forgotten." Ben says.

"We can make sure that doesn't happen to us." Deke replies.

"How can we do that?" Joe asks.

"Come with me." Deke replies.

"Where?" Joe asks.

"Backstage!" Deke replies.

The group goes backstage and grab their instruments and prepare to take the stage. The audience was shocked to hear the The Cromactics are performing today. The Cromactics take the stage to sing an old New Orleans cut 'When the saints come marching in'. As they perform Pazzaz looks on with envy.

Especially when The Cromactics got a big round of applause. Much bigger than what Pazzaz received.

"Look at that. we got a standing ovation." Ben says.

"Yeah, I guess we're not dead yet." Joe replies.

"Not by a long shot." Clyde says.

Meanwhile outside in the audience.

"Did you see that, James? They got a bigger applause than we did." John says.

"So, they are trying to compete with us after all. That was a mistake they shouldn't have made."

"What are you gonna do James?" John asks.

"Come on, follow me"

Backstage, The Cromactics are celebrating their success. Clyde and Deke want to go out to a club but the rest of The Cromactics don't feel up to hanging out. So, Clyde and Deke head for the club. James and John follow them. Clyde and Deke arrive at the club and look for a young lady named Marilyn Ruiz. They couldn't find her there so they decide to head for the malt shop. Only to be ambushed by four guys. It seems that one guy happens to be the big brother of Marilyn and he thinks Deke, is the one that was dogging her out, and beating on her. The situation gets ugly as Deke, tries to explain he has the wrong man. But he did not want to listen to reasoning. Big Al takes a swing at Deke, hitting him in the mouth knocking him off balance. Clyde hits big Al, in the jaw, knocking him off balance. Next, two guys jump, Clyde. A fourth guy runs up on, Deke. As he's getting up, but he flips the guy over and he lands on top of a table hitting the floor rolling under another table. Big Al, regroups and comes after Deke, who delivers a double combination to the jaw knocking him down and out. Clyde, flips man no. 2 over the bar as guy no. 3 takes a swing at him and misses. Clyde hits him with a left to the gut and a right to the jaw knocking him out.

Deke walks over to guy no. 4 and kicks him in the chin knocking him out. Clyde, spots James and John overlooking the crowd.

"You alright, Clyde?"

"I'm cool. I needed the work out."

"I wonder why they thought I was banging the hell out of Marilyn?"

"I'll give you two guesses."

"What?"

"James and John!"

"Where?"

"Over there!"

"What the hell are they doing here?"

"I don't know, but let's go find out." Deke and Clyde walk over to James and John.

"What are you two doing here?" Clyde asks.

"Last time I checked this was a free country."

"Yeah, we can go anywhere we want to." John says.

"Did yall see what just happened to us?"

"Yeah, Deke, we saw it. I guess you guys got a few enemies in Tucson." James replies.

"Funny we didn't have any till you guys got here." Clyde says.

"Are you insinuating that we had something to do with that little brawl you had?"

"You dam right?" Clyde replies to James.

"Fellas, fellas, I assure you that we had nothing to do with it." James says.

"Bullshit!" Clyde replies.

"Temper Temper, Clyde. we don't want you to bust a blood vessel by being too hyper." James says.

"You try to be so subtle with your bullshit James. But you know what I see right through you." Deke replies.

"So, you think you know me huh, Deke?"

"Oh yeah, I know all about you. I know you don't like us being here first before you. I know you didn't like the ladies applauding for us more than they did for you. I know you don't like the fact we get standing ovations when we perform, and you don't. "Deke, replies as James, starts to get mad. "I know you don't like the fact that a girl like Susan, likes a guy like me, but loathes a guy like you."

"Hey James, you gonna let him get away with that?"

"Why don't you shut up?" Clyde says.

"Why don't you make me?" John asks.

Clyde punches John in the jaw knocking him back up against the bar. James jumps up to sneak, Clyde, but Deke throws a roundhouse kick at James, in his gut knocking him back in his seat. John gets up and rushes Clyde then decks him to the canvass. Clyde, rolls over and back kicks John, in the stomach knocking him back against the bar. While Deke's, back is turned James, hits Deke, with a football tackle, knocking him up against the bar. Deke, elbows James, in the nose twice catching him off guard. Then he elbows him in the chin dropping him to his knees. Clyde punches John in the mouth with a two-piece dropping him. Deke, kicks James, in the jaw with a swift low roundhouse to the left side of his face. The bartender calls the police and within 5 minutes they arrived and arrested everybody. Including the 4 guys that jumped Deke and Clyde. The police separated the 4 guys from, James, and John who were separated from Deke and Clyde. Deke and Clyde were escorted to the Sargent's office while everyone else was escorted to a cell.

"The Sargent will be in soon. make yourselves comfortable." Cop no.1 says.

"Thank you!" Deke says hopping in a chair and putting his feet up on the Sargent's desk.

"Man, I ain't never been in jail before."

"that's makes two of us, Clyde."

"What do you think they'll do to us?"

"I don't know. "The Sargent walks in!

"Gentlemen, how are you?" Sg. ask.

"Fine Sg." Clyde replies.

"Now I know you two weren't roughing up everybody in one of my clubs, were you? I mean I just know you two musicians from Jersey weren't causing a problem in my club?"

"Oh no we weren't Sg." Deke replies.

"Young man, kindly take your feet off my desk."

"Oh------sorry!"

"Now------tell me what happened."

"Well, we went into the club to have a good time. We knew this girl that supposed to work there, but when we asked around, we were told she wasn't working there tonight. So, we were on our way out to the malt shop when 4 guys jumped us. They thought, Deke was the guy that was beating up on the girl we we're looking for."

"So, as I see it you destroyed public property over a girl?"

"No! it was a misunderstanding. and we were only defending ourselves."

"Did you two have anything to drink?"

"No!" Deke replies.

"You sure?"

"Yes, Sg."

"You are mighty hyper not to be under the influence."

"Like you said, two musicians from Jersey. We are always hyper. It's how we feel rock-n-roll."

"You're a wise ass aren't you son?"

"So, I'm told!"

"What's your name?"

"Deke Rivers!"

"Mr. Rivers, I got a little test for you. "The Sg. says holding up 3 fingers. "How many fingers do you, see?"

"5!"

"5?"

"Yeah, 3 standing up and 2 folded down." Deke replies, laughing.

"Very funny! You two are beginning to annoy me. You destroyed public property."

"I told you we were defending ourselves."

"Oh, you were?"

"Yes!"

"And what is your name."

"Clyde Simmons!"

"Well, Mr. Simmons I have a witness who said you struck the first blow. You and Mr. Rivers."

"We were provoked!"

"Oh-----now you were provoked. fellas I can charge you with assault and battery and destroying public property. At your ages that'll get yall 2 months in juvenile detention with 6-month probation."

Soon a female cop walks into the office.

"Here's that report on that bar incident you wanted, Sg."

"Thank you, Miss McClanahan."

Deke and Clyde eyes light up and they quickly stand up.

"Hello, my name is Deke."

"And my name is, Clyde. How are you?"

"I'm fine!"

"I never saw a policewoman that looked as pretty as you." Deke replies.

"I'll bet you say that to everybody."

"No, just to you!"

"He's right, you are a very nice-looking young lady.'"

"Thank you! I love to chat with yall but I got a lot of work to do so if you will excuse me I'll see yall later."

"I hope so!" Deke replies.

"Bye!"

"Bye!" They replied.

"She's out of yall league fellas."

"Heh, heh, heh, no girls' out of my league."

"So sure, of yourself aren't you, Mr. Rivers?"

"Always!"

"Well, you best be more concern about these charges against you than your libido."

"Those are bogus charges. We didn't destroy anything." Deke, says.

"That's not what I heard."

"Well, you heard wrong."

"I don't think so Mr. Rivers."

"You don't think so? Who told you could think?"

"You're treading a thin line Mr. Rivers."

"Wait, why aren't, James and John in here?"

"Oh, we let them go a half hour ago. I released them personally before I came up here to talk to you two."

"Why did you release them?"

"They were the victims of you two."

"But they started it."

"So, Mr. Simmons you are saying they're the cause of those 4 guys provoking you into a fight?"

"Yes!"

"Do you have proof?"

"No!"

"Then your guilty as charged."

"Sarge a man just posted bail for these two gangsters." Cop no 2, replies.

"Hey I resent that." Clyde says.

"You'll get over it. Who posted bail for them?"

"Mr. MacDonald! "Clyde and Deke look at each other smiling.

"He's on line 2 for you Sarge."

"Oh shit!"

The Sargent picks up the phone and talks to Mr. MacDonald. He's not too pleased with the conversation he's having.

"Mr. Simmons, Mr. Rivers, you're free to go."

"We are?" Deke, asks.

"What about the charges?"

"Mr. MacDonald got the bartender to drop the charges against you. So, by law you're free to go."

"Cool, let's split!" Deke, says.

"But remember this, if this happens again, I will make sure you get 30 days in my cell downstairs.

That's 30 days each. No musician is gonna ruin my town. Have I made myself clear?"

"Yes, you have. And might I say you have been a very pleasant host and very gracious."

"Oh really?"

"Yeah! You didn't let us spend 1 minute in a cell. You had us here in the company of your presence."

"You know Mr. Rivers you are really pushing it. Mr. Simmons, get this guy out of here before I change my mind."

"We gone Sargent!"

Mr. MacDonald is outside waiting for Deke and Clyde. They head back to the ranch where Connie and Susan are outside waiting for Deke and Clyde.

"Deke, are you alright?" Susan asks hugging him.

"I'm fine!"

"I couldn't believe you were arrested." Susan says.

"You couldn't, I was there, and I still don't believe it." Clyde replies.

"Yall don't look beat up." Connie says.

"That's because we weren't." Clyde replies.

"Hmm, sounds good you guys are good fighters as well as singers." Connie says.

"How did this happen?" Susan asks.

"I was mistaken for a guy who beat up a girl that I happen to know and asked about in the club."

"Yeah, but you had help"

"Yeah, James and john were there."

"They sent those guys after us."

"Why?"

"Jealousy! Pazzaz doesn't like the billing we have here." Deke replies.

"Especially, Mr. Coburn."

"Yeah, he really is all into himself."

"He can't stand a little competition."

"Even if it ain't no competition."

"But he's so paranoid that he thinks everybody is a threat to him."

"I can't stand him or his band." Connie says.

"What are yall gonna do? It seems to me; James would stop at nothing to get what he wants."
Susan asks.

"Well for one, we're gonna watch our backs." Deke replies.

"What's not right! Those clowns shouldn't be doing this to you. it's not fair. And that, James Coburn, he's too egotistical, self-centered, arrogant conceited, stuck up. That man is such a roole. He's a louse, a cad, and a bore. He wants to be the best, but he'll never be if he doesn't come down off his high horse. If he thinks anyone is gonna fall for him, he's got another thing coming. "Connie says.

"I couldn't agree with you more, Connie." Deke, says, kissing Connie, on her forehead.

"It's been a long day. Deke, I'm turning in. I'll see yall tomorrow." Clyde says.

"I think we all should be going to bed." Deke replies.

"I love that idea." Connie says smiling.

"Come on I'll walk yall to your room." Deke, replies putting his arms around Connie and Susan, walking them back to their rooms.

CHAPTER 7

On the day of the clambake the group perform a special request at the theatre. They got many reviews for performing 'teddy bear'! That they were asked to do it again. As they perform, Pazzaz looks on in discomfort. They can't stand the publicity and hype The Cromatics are getting. So, the group comes up with a plan to distort The Cromactics. The Cromatics will be performing later at the clambake. So, the group thought of competing with them at the clambake. They figure they would get back at them by performing in their hour as they did in Pazzaz's hour. At the clambake, the girls are helping with the menu by cooking a lot of chicken, fish, shrimp, lobsters, and clams. The group comes out to sing 'Clambake'. after their performance, Pazzaz comes out to sing. The group doesn't get too many listeners as everyone's busy doing their own thing now that; The Cromatics have finished their performance. Pazzaz don't look too happy as it looks as though they are being ignored. James storms off in rage back to his barracks as the rest of the group follows. Later, Deke meets up with, Vivian and her sister Maria and they hang out by a stream in the back of the fair grounds of the clambake. To, Deke's surprise the girls tell him how attracted they are to him. And Deke, says the feelings are mutual. Now the threesome discusses getting together and having sex with each other. The three-sneak back to girls' barracks where they perform their sexual fantasy. When, Deke's finished he slips out their room where he runs into Joe, coming out of, Talisa's room. The last time they ran into each other like this, Deke was with, Courtney, and Joe was with, Diane. Talisa, comes out and invites, Deke in as, Vivian, invites Joe in. 6 hours later the guys come out tired and staggering back to their rooms.

CHAPTER 8

The next day Sondra and some of the girls are discussing, Clyde.

"So, are you and Clyde, going out tonight?" Pat, asks.

"Yes, we are." Sondra replies.

"Let me guess, you're going to the malt shop?"

"I don't know where he's taking me, Pat."

"I'll bet it's the malt shop."

"You like him a lot don't you, Sondra?" Careta asks.

"Yes, I do!"

"But the question is does he feel the same way about you?"

"Yes, he does! And you know I won the bet."

"No, you haven't."

"Yes, I have! I got him interested in me."

"Yes, but he doesn't have feelings for you like you have for him."

"I'm telling you he does."

"Yeah, we'll see!"

"You know you put too much into this. Do you have some special interest in him yourself?"

"Yeah, I wonder about that myself." Dianne says.

"Oh no girlfriend, you can't turn this around on me. I think, Clyde is cute an all but, I'm interested in, Ben. I don't want to see, Clyde, get hurt by you."

"I'm not gonna hurt him, Pat. I'll admit at first this started out as a game. An ego thing you might say. But I actually like, Clyde. He is a lot of fun to be with. I hope this could grow into something."

"I suppose!"

Across at the boy's barracks, Ben gets a hold of a football and The Cromatics play a game of touch football. Susan, Connie, Courtney and Sonja act as cheerleaders. During the game The Cromatics break in a song titled 'Come on everybody do the kick'. Later, that night. Clyde and Sondra enjoy a night out at the malt shop.

"You know Pat, said you might bring me here."

"She must've read my mind. Does she know how much I like you?"

"No but why don't you tell me."

"Okay! Sondra, I enjoy spending time with you. I have grown very fond of you."

"I like you too, Clyde."

"I'm glad to hear that." Soon Pat, comes over and sits down with Clyde and Sondra.

"Hi yall doing?" Pat, asks.

"I'm fine." Clyde replies.

"What are you doing here, Pat?"

"Having a malt!"

"Very funny! I mean what are you doing here with us?"

"Oh, I came to say hi and to see how you two love birds are doing."

"Oh, I'm doing great. I was just telling, Sondra how much I like her."

"Ah you fallen for her?"

"Oh yes! I'm head over heels for this girl."

"Well, Sondra, you were right. I guess you did win the bet."

"Bet? What bet?"

"Ooops! Did I say bet? I ------ I was referring to a little minor------minor thing that really isn't all that important now that I think about it."

"Sondra, what bet is she talking about?"

"Uh------well-----you heard her, it really isn't important."

"What bet are you talking about, Pat?"

"Well-------it's about you and Sondra."

"What about us-------Sondra?"

"Well------I bet, Pat that I can get any guy interested in me. So, I decided on you when I saw you. But that's only because I liked you when I first saw you."

"All this time you were just playing with me?"

"No------I wasn't playing, I really do like you."

"Yeah, sure you do."

"No------I'm serious------I do like you, Clyde."

"This wasn't for real, none of it. It was all a game to you. A bet is all you had to interest you in me."

"No, it isn't like that. I can explain it to you."

"Oh, you can?"

"Yes, I can!"

"You can explain you coming on to me, kissing me, hugging me, putting your arms around me, holding me, caressing me, fondling me. Telling me how much you like me, how much you care about me. And how much you want to be with me. You can explain all that?"

"Now I think about it, it would be hard to explain."

"That's what I thought------I'm gone." Clyde says, getting up and leaving the malt shop.

"Clyde, wait!"

Clyde heads back to the ranch to get away from, Sondra.

CHAPTER 9

The next day, Jill, Sonja, Careta, Pat and Dianne discuss what happened with Sondra and Clyde.

"I hate to rub it in, but someone messed up on the road to romance Careta, says.

"Don't start, Careta. I'm not in the mood. You don't have to rub it in." Sondra says.

"Why not? You got what you deserve, and you know it." Careta says.

"Girls, we shouldn't blame, Sondra." Pat, says.

"Right, we should blame you for opening your big mouth." Sondra replies.

"One would say you are the cause of their breakup." Jill says.

"Oh please! You're not gonna put this off on me." Pat, replies.

"She's right! I started this; it's my fault. and I have to correct it." Sondra says.

"How are you gonna do that?" Dianne asks.

"I haven't figured that part out yet."

"You'll have to talk to him." Sonja says.

"I will if he'll listen. Last night he didn't return my calls."

"You'll have to do this face to face." Sonja says.

"Easier said than done." Dianne replies.

"Yeah, he's gotta be willing to listen to, Sondra." Careta says.

"Clyde, must be going through something right now." Jill replies.

"Shoot, so am I"

"Yeah, but you're not taking this as hard as, Clyde." Jill replies.

"How do you know how hard I'm taking it?" Sondra asks.

"I can see the symptoms."

"Bull!" Sondra says.

"Look if you want, Clyde back you're gonna have to talk to him." Sonja replies.

"It is the only way." Dianne says.

"But he won't talk to me."

"Don't take no for an answer." Careta says.

"Yeah, you're good at that." Pat, replies.

"Thanks a lot!"

"Look the bottom line is, if you want, Clyde, back you're gonna have to talk to him. Whether he wants to hear it or not." Pat, replies. Soon a knock comes at the door.

"Come in!" Pat, says.

"Hello, girls, it's just me." Deke replies. "How are yall?"

"We're fine!" Sonja replies.

"All except one." Pat, says.

"Let me guess, Sondra?"

"You got it." Pat, replies.

"I guess you heard?" Sondra asks.

"Yeah! Clyde, is highly upset."

"I know, I know! I am sorry, I do like him, really I do------but he won't listen to me."

"Don't worry, he just needs some time to think."

"He really hates me."

" No, he doesn't. He doesn't hate you."

"You talk to him?"

"No!"

"So how do you know?"

"I know, Clyde. relax, he'll come around. I know he wants to know why you did what you did. So when you tell him, he'll feel a lot better."

"I hope so."

"Do you need anything?"

"Yeah, Clyde!"

"Anything else?"

"No!"

"Okay! Well, I'll be getting back; you hang in there, Sondra. everything's gonna be all-right. I promise!" Deke says, kissing, Sondra on her forehead. "Goodbye!"

"Bye!" They all reply."

"We'll be here for you, Sondra." Sonja says.

"We'll see you through this." Pat, replies.

"No matter what, we're here for you." Careta says.

"Including me!" Jill replies.

"And me!" Dianne says.

"I'm glad to hear that, cause I really do need yall." Sondra replies.

"Well, we're here." Dianne says.

Meanwhile, Ben and Mike catch up with, Clyde and they try to talk him into talking to, Sondra. After a couple of hours of badgering, Clyde, they moved him to thinking about talking to, Sondra. In Sly's room, Sonja is there to spend a romantic evening with the man of her dreams. They discuss their future as, Sonja says she is going to college to pursue her career in acting. She also has plans to major in computer science.

The subject of Clyde and Sondra comes up. Meanwhile, Deke is with Connie and Susan singing a song titled "Tender Feeling." Across the hall, Sondra sits up in her room when Clyde comes by.

"Hey, someone's at the door." Pat, says.

"So, tell them to come in." Careta replies.

"Come in!" Pat, yells.

"Hi! am I interrupting yall?" Clyde asks.

Everybody eyes light up as, Clyde, walks in the room.

"Hi, Clyde! How are you?" Pat, asks.

"I've been better."

"I'll bet! C'mon girls let's leave these two alone." Pat, says.

The girls leave while Sondra and Clyde talk.

"I'm glad to see you, Clyde."

"Are you?"

"Yes------I am!"

"You want to explain to me about your little bet with, Pat?"

"Yes! I shot off my mouth to the other girls on how I don't need to show interest in a man. But I can get him to show interest in me. It started off to be a game, but as we gotten to know each other, I started to like you. I truly do like you. I fell head over heels for you too. I am sorry if you felt you was being used. I would take it back if I could, but I can't. I wish you could forgive me."

"I forgive you. just don't do that again."

"I won't!" Sondra, says, hugging and kissing, Clyde.
Meanwhile, Deke heads over to, Dianne's room as James steps into Susan and Connie's room.

"James!" Susan says.

"Susan, did you miss me?"

"No!"

"Come on! I know you're not gonna act like you don't like me?"

"Not that again!"

"That kiss should have said it all."

"Well, it didn't!"

"Kiss?" Connie asks.

"You're playing hard to get again. Are you nervous?"

"Not really!"

"You won't allow yourself to feel what you feel for me."

"Uh------did I miss something?" Connie asks.

"No!"

"Oh, go on, tell your sister how much chemistry we got going on here."

"You are sick!"

"So, I'm told!"

"Susan, you want to clear this up for me?"

"Later!"

"Yeah, now we're busy."

Deke walks in.

"James, why are you here?"

"I'm here on business with, Susan."

"Oh, you do?"

"Yes! I guess you should know how much your girl likes me."

"Really?"

"Really! She denies it but, I know she wants me deep down inside."

"Is he for real?" Connie asks.

"I think so." Deke replies.

"You plan to do something?" James asks.

"Nah! Susan, got this,"

"James, I don't like you, never have, never will. I'm not denying any feelings for you because there is none. I wouldn't be with you if you were the last louse on earth."

"Ooo that hurts!" Deke, says.

"You ain't all that, nor will you ever be."

"That's telling him!" Deke, says.

"You need help, James. Because you're sick and twisted and stupid."

"Strike 2, James!" Deke, says.

"Oh, it's like that?" James asks.

"Yes!" Everyone replies.

"No one talks to, James like that and gets away with it." James says raising his hand.

"Uh, James I wouldn't do that." Deke, says.

"Why not? You're too far away to do anything to me. So, what can happen?"

Susan hits, James in the ribs with her elbow.

"You'll regret doing that. All of you will."

"Hmm, more threats? Connie!"

Deke winks at, Connie as she grabs, James's arm and pins it behind his back. Then she rushes him to the door as, Deke opens it, and Connie, pushes him out.

"I like yall style." Deke, says, hi fiving the girls. "Together, there's nothing we can't do." Deke, says, hugging and kissing the girls.

CHAPTER 10

The next day The Cromactics are at the theatre. Deke, asks, Careta to join them again to do the same song they did before, "Hey Little Girl". Careta, was flattered, Deke asks her back again. She agreed to do the song with them. After their performance, the group retires back to their barracks while Deke and Careta return to her room.

"I must say you are a good dancer, Careta."

"Thank you! And I must say you have good moves and vibrations."

"Thank you!"

"You know this is the first time we have been alone together since you've been here."

"I know! I hope you don't think I was avoiding you or something?"

"Oh, I know you wasn't. I know how busy you are. Especially since you have been with a lot of the girls here, especially, Susan."

"Well, Susan is a wonderful girl. I like her a lot."

"Oh, is it serious between you two?"

"Not------really! We won't be seeing each other for good while once we leave so, we haven't made any commitments."

"Oh, I see!" Careta says, putting her arms around, Deke.

"Uh--------Careta, do I detect some physical attraction here?"

"Uh-------huh!" Careta, replies, kissing, Deke.

"Has anyone ever told you, you have very, very soft lips?"

"No! Nobody has ever told me that."

"Well, I'm telling you. you have very, very, soft lips."

"Thank you!"

"You also have very smooth, lovely, skin."

"Thank you!"

"It's kinda like the complexion of brown sugar."

"Oh!"

"Yes! and brown sugar is very pretty to look at and very delicious to taste and to eat. Which you definitely are very delicious." Deke, says kissing, Careta on the lips, her face and her neck.

"Hmm, it is true what they say about you."

"And what is that?"

"You are a very charming young man."

"Thank you!"

"You have such poise and grace to you. That makes you every bit as smooth and suave, a debonair type of guy. I must say you are a very cool type of guy. You are very polite and very gallant. With all those qualities, that makes you a very, very, very sexy guy."

"Thank you! I'm flattered you think so highly of me."

"I only speak the truth."

"Of course, you know you are a very sexy young lady?"

"I don't know, but I'll take your word for it."

"You know I am attracted to you."

"The feelings mutual."

"So, what should we do about this."

"What do you want to do about it?"

Deke, kisses, Careta, then picks her up and carries her over to the bed and gently lays her down and then he lays down on top of her. After six hours, Deke leaves,

Careta's room only to run into, Pat and Joe who just finished spending an evening together. Pat and Deke glaze into each other's eyes and a spark goes on. Deke goes into, Pat's room as, Joe goes into, Careta's room as she motions him to come in. Six hours later, Deke, and Joe come out the rooms only to run into, Susan, who just happened to take a stroll because she couldn't sleep. She is a little upset to see, Deke coming out of, Pat's room at 4:30 in the morning. She didn't have to ask what was, Deke doing. She kinda figured that out already. She just looked at, Deke and ran back to her room. Deke, went after her but she locked the door as she went in. She refused to open the door for, Deke. she refused to talk to Deke. Deke, tried to explain but, Susan refused to listen. Deke, finally gave up and went back to his barracks and told, Joe what happened. For the next 2 days, Deke has been trying to get in contact with, Susan. but she won't talk to him. Every time he knocks on her door; she would open it and slam the door in his face. So, he tries the telephone. But every time she picks up the phone and she heard his voice, she'd slam the phone in his ear. If they saw each other in the street, Susan would cross the street. It's July 28th. The Cromactics will be leaving in 4 days. After all that has happened, Deke doesn't want to leave with, Susan mad at him. Susan isn't only not speaking to, Deke, she isn't speaking to, Pat either. Or Careta! James and his band found out about, Susan and Deke's little squabble. James, thinks he has the chance to get with, Susan if he can console her and persuade her from ever giving, Deke another chance with her. Susan does a good job of being distant from everyone, including, Connie. Connie tries to comfort her, but she doesn't seem to have much luck doing it. She tells, Susan she should talk to, Deke and see what he has to say about what happened. Susan's, reply is it's too painful to talk to, Deke. Now she knows there's no commitment between her and Deke. So, he is free to see other girls and do whatever.

That's what hurts so much. She wants to be the only girl; Deke can spend time with. But that's not the situation because he has been with other girls. That means he's not happy being with just her. Maybe those other girls he likes better than her. She's afraid if she talks to, Deke he'll tell her that. So, to keep it from hurting so much, she just won't talk to him. But Connie says she's gonna have to talk to Deke so she can find out the whole story and stop assuming. She owes, Deke that much to listen to him.

The next night, James, and John make their move on the girls, Sonja, Sondra, Sue, Susan, Connie, Pat, and Careta. John tries his luck with Sonja, but she is not interested in him since she is with, Sly. John can't understand what she sees in, Sly. But Sonja, assures him he shouldn't be concerned about, Sly because he would never have a chance with her even if she wasn't with, Sly. Sly is a nice, suave, decent. loving, young man who knows how to treat a lady. These are qualities, John lacks. Sonja's, sister, Sue agrees with her. A couple of other members in James's band meets up with them, but they get nowhere with, Sondra and Sue. Pat and Careta have no time for, James and his boys either. Now, James tries to talk to, Susan. he's willing to forget that little incident that happened with him and the girls, because he sees that, Susan is in pain. And she looks like she could use a shoulder to cry on. But Susan quickly let's, James knows she doesn't need anything from him. Now, James wants to try to dog, Deke but Susan she quickly comes to his defense since he is everything a girl could ask for in a guy. Everything, James is not. James didn't like to be humiliated. again, in front of witnesses.

Susan chumps him off, then leaves. And the rest of the girls follow behind her, leaving Pazzaz standing with their mouths open looking dumbfounded. James was furious.

Susan has dissed him once too many times. now he's out for revenge. He wants to get even with, Connie, Susan, and The Cromatics. He feels he's been too soft, now he has to show everybody what, James Coburn is made of.

CHAPTER 11

The next day, Susan, and Connie are in their room talking until, Pat and Careta come in.

"So, Susan, when are you gonna talk to, Deke?"

"I don't know, Connie. I'm afraid of what he might tell me.

"Susan!" Connie says putting her arm around Susan. "You'll never know unless you talk to him. personally, I don't think that is the case with him."

"You really think he likes me?"

"I know he does."

"And we can vouch for that." Pat says as she and Careta enter the room. "Girl let me tell you, Deke is a wonderful, loving, sexy guy. But he does love the ladies.

"And I can second that." Careta replies.

"But he does like you."

"He told me personally, he's very fond of you."

"And we have no reason to think he would lie."

"And neither do you."

"He did say yall didn't have any commitments with each other."

"Which is why he spent time with us."

"But it wasn't because he didn't like you."

"Or because he liked us better,"

"He didn't know you felt this strongly about him."

"And he still doesn't know."

"Because you haven't told him."

"And you should."

"Because he deserves to know."

"You know he has feelings too."

"But you didn't stop to consider that------"

"------did you?" They both ask.

"No------I didn't. But you're right. I should talk to him. I'll bet he's mad at me now because he hasn't called me today. Which is odd since he's been calling me for the past 3 days. But not today. I haven't considered his feelings at all. I wonder what he's feeling right now."

At the theatre The Cromatics are performing a recently composed tune titled, "I Gotta Find My Baby". It fits the mood that; Deke has been in for the past few days. Now he's expressing his feelings in a song.

Susan, Connie, Pat and Careta come in the theatre as The Cromatics come out of there music breakdown and sing the last verse of the song. Susan, gaze into, Deke's eyes as she listens to the lyrics in the song. After their performance, Susan rushes backstage to talk to, Deke.

"Good job, Deke." Sly, says.

"Thanks, Sly."

"Hey, you really belt it out there." Joe says.

"Thanks, Joe!"

"Hey, Susan's out there."

"She's always out there, Clyde."

"No, I mean she's coming this way."

"She's coming back here?"

"Yeah, Deke, she's coming backstage."

"Your prayers have been answered." Joe says.

"Hello, Deke!"

"Hello, Susan!"

"How are you?"

"Fine I suppose!"

"Look I want to apologize for not speaking to you."

"I take it you have very strong feelings for me."

"Yes, I do! I just jumped to all sorts of conclusions when I thought------well when I saw you with, Pat. I thought you didn't like me since you were with those other girls."

"Don't be silly of course I like you."

"Well------I thought you didn't. I also thought you liked them better than me. That's why I didn't speak to you because I thought you was gonna tell me that. Since we didn't have any commitments."

"No, Susan there's nobody I like more than you."

"I know that now. I know this sounds silly but, I don't want you to spend time with anybody else, but me."

"Hmm------can I think about that?"

"Yes!"

"Come here girl!" Deke, says hugging, Susan.

"You know, Pat and Careta told me what you said about me. I want you to know I am very fond of you too."

"I'm glad to hear that. Listen we gotta pack our stuff so I'll see you back at the ranch."

"Okay!"

Deke goes outside to join the group while, Susan joins, Connie outside up front. Pazzaz is outside moving in. The group goes inside while, James stays outside waiting for Connie and Susan. Susan and Connie reroute their direction and go out towards the back with, Deke. only, Deke enters the side door and comes back into the theatre as the girls go outside to the back. James follows the girls out back.

"Well, I guess we can always wait till, Deke comes out, Connie."

"There's no need for that ladies."

"James!" Connie says.

"In the flesh!"

"I thought we got rid of you." Susan says.

"Think again!"

"James, you best leave us alone or so help me God I will------"

"You will what, Connie? Put my arm behind my back again? Huh? Well, there won't be no more of that shit, ever." James, says slapping Connie, knocking her down and out.

"Oh my God! What have you done to her?"

"Oh, she'll be alright. Which is more than I can say for you."

"What?" Susan asks fearfully.

"Oh, you don't think I forgot that cheap shot to the ribs you gave me?" James, says grabbing, Susan by her arm.

"Well, I really wasn't thinking about it."

"I'll bet! You seem to have a lot to say about me when your friends are around."

"Well, I meant every word of it."

"Oh, I'm sorry you said that." James, says twisting, Susan's arm.

"Ouch! Stop! You're hurting me."

"That's the whole idea."

Deke hears some noise outside, so he goes outside to investigate.

"James, stop let go of me?" Susan yells kicking and hitting, James.

"Susan, if you don't stop fighting me I will------"

"You will what?" Deke, asks.

"This!" James replies slapping Susan.

"Susan!" Deke, yells as he races towards, James. he jumps up and fly kicks, James in the face knocking him down.

"Susan you alright?"

"No! Keep him away from me. I gotta help, Connie."

"Connie? What happened to her?"

"James, knocked her out."

"You take care of her. I'll take care of, James."

"I see this is what it comes down too."

"Yeah, James! You think you are the best at whatever you do. Let's see if that's true."

"Fine let's do this."

James takes a swing at, Deke, but misses because, Deke steps back a few feet. James swings at Deke Again, but he ducks and James misses, Deke punches James, in the jaw dropping him. Deke stands over, James as, James sits up on the ground looking up at him. Meanwhile, Jim sneaks outside and sees James and Deke, with his back to him. So, Jim sneaks up behind him, James sees what, Jim, is doing. He's about to strike when Deke jumps up and roundhouse kick Jim in the face knocking him down and out. James, rushes, Deke from behind, but Deke, plants his left leg firmly on the ground then whips his right leg up and around hitting, James in his jaw knocking him up against a car. James, look in amazement because he wonders how Deke knew, Jim was behind him. Deke, tells him how it seem strange that, James got real quiet and he kept looking behind him. Then he heard footsteps behind him. After that it was all timing. James was furious so he rushed, Deke again knocking him in a pile of garbage. James goes to punch, Deke but he blocks it, then knees him in the stomach twice, and delivers a right to the jaw twice. Then flips him over and he jumps on top of James and starts punching him in the face. Jim, wakes up and rushes Deke, only to catch a backhand to the jaw knocking him off balance. Now Deke, grabs, Jim picks him up over his shoulders spinning him around and slams him on top of a car. James gets up and punches Deke in the jaw knocking him up against the car. Then he picks, Deke up, and throws him over the car. Meanwhile inside the theatre The Cromatics are having it out with the rest of Pazzaz. Sly, is fighting, John and is enjoying beating the crap out of John. The funny thing about it, he's talking to him while he's beating him up. Sly, didn't like the way, John came on to, Sonja. so, he's letting him know he didn't like the way he disrespected, Sonja. Sly, hits him with 4 different combinations to the jaw sending him flying across the stage. John gets up and punches, Sly knocking him back against the wall. Sly, laughs in John's face as, John swings and misses and Sly punches him in the stomach and grabs him and slams him in the wall. Then kicks him in the back. Meanwhile outside, Deke rushes, James slamming him up against the car. Deke, grabs, James and James, grabs, Deke and they throw each other up against the car. Deke, knees, James in the groan and slams him up against the car then throw him on the ground.

James, gets up but, Deke drop kicks, James to the ground. Then he punches James splitting his mouth open. James surrenders as the police come. Deke, grabs, James and walk him inside the theatre where, Sly is stomping on, John. The police pull, Sly off John and take Pazzaz, The Cromatics, Sonja, Sue, Careta, Dianne, Pat, Jill, Sondra, Connie and Susan down to the station. The cop escorts everyone except, Pazzaz to the Sg.'s office. The cop tells everyone to make themselves comfortable and Deke does just that by hopping in the chair and putting his feet on the Sg.'s desk. Connie does the same. Clyde, reminds, Deke about the last time he did that. And so did the cop. but, Deke doesn't care and does it anyway. The Sg. comes in and is astonished at all the people he sees in his office.

"Well, well, well, look at what we have here. Now let's see there was a big brawl in the theatre.

And it involved all of you. My we haven't had this much excitement since------" the sg. pauses looking at, Deke. " Oh no its you again."

"Yes, Sg. it's me again." Deke, replies smiling.

"Are these people friends of yours?"

"Yes! This is the rest of the band. And the ladies are our friends."

"Uh huh------you're Mr. Rivers, correct?"

"Yes!"

"And you're Mr. Simmons, correct?"

"Yes!"

"Man got a good memory."

"Oh, I always remember troublemakers".

"Is that what we are?"

"Mr. Rivers?"

"Yes!"

"Why are your feet on my desk again?"

"The officer said for us to make ourselves comfortable, so I did." Deke says turning to, Connie laughing.

"Now who might this pretty young lady be?"

"This is, Connie."

"And why are her feet on my desk?"

"She wanted to be comfortable too, so she did what came natural." Deke, replies smiling while slapping, Connie 's hand.

"How nice well I'm telling both of you to get your feet off my desk."

"Oh, come on Sg. My boots are clean. There's no dirt on them."

"There's nothing but dirt in Tucson."

"I know but look my feet are on the desk. They're not touching your papers."

"I don't care if your feet were on the file cabinets. Get them off my desk"

"Dam, no sense of humor." Connie says.

"None whatsoever." Deke replies.

"You shouldn't be harassing us." Connie says.

"Young lady, I haven't done anything to you, yet."

"Why are we here?" Mike, asks.

"For disturbing the peace. Not to mention destroying public property, assault and battery."

"What did we destroy? We were fighting in the street." Deke replies.

"And we didn't destroy anything on the stage." Sly, says.

"Or backstage!" Mike replies.

"Regardless! You still were fighting in a public place. You know we didn't have this problem till you musicians came here."

"You mean till Pazzaz came here." Mike replies.

"I mean both of yall. now I know there's a rivalry going on between yall. Which is typical among musicians. Yall always in competition with each other. And as always you wind up in a fighting match with each other. First, it's at the club, now the theatre. You guys have become the talk of the town. I never liked the idea of you young rock n roll rebels coming into my town to perform in the first place. But the mayor doesn't mind so what am I to do? But look at how yall repay him. Those group of bandit's downstairs are a bunch of troublemakers. I see that. But they aint gonna cause any more trouble in my town again. I'll see to that."

"What about us?" Mike, asks.

"Oh, you guys seem to be heroes in this story."

"We are?" Ben asks.

"Yes!"

"I don't believe it." Ben says.

"Neither do I, but that's what they say."

"I'll bet Pazzaz won't like that either."

"They didn't! Unfortunately, their agent bailed them out."

"So, they get off just like that?" Joe asks.

"What are you complaining about? So are you!"

"So, are we?"

"You mean, we can go?" Pat, asks.

"Yes! It's against my better judgement, but as some of you may already know, Mr. MacDonald got the charges dropped against you."

"You knew that when you came in here?" Greg asks.

"Yes!"

"So why didn't you tell us?" Sonja asks.

"Because I have the right to remain silent."

"Oh, you're a comedian." Clyde says.

"No, but your friend is. Now get out of my office. All of you."

Everyone gets up and leave the sg. office. Deke, Sly, Clyde and Connie go downstairs to see what's going on with Pazzaz.

"Now what do yall want?" Cop no. 1 asks.

"We came to see Pazzaz." Sly replies.

"For what?"

"We're curious!" Deke replies.

"Oh, you want to rub it in."

"Rub what in?" Deke replies.

"Pazzaz is out of here."

"What do you mean?" Clyde asks.

"As soon as they are bailed out, they gotta go."

"Why?" Connie asks.

"You gotta ask? You remember what, James did to you don't you?"

"Yeah!"

"Well, the town of Tucson has band the group from performing here. The city doesn't want no part of them."

The group comes out of the office and stop to talk to The Cromatics.

"We heard yall were leaving." Deke, says.

"We are!" James replies.

"So, what's stopping you?" Clyde asks.

"Look, I wanted to take one last look at all."

"Why? So, you can put a hex on us?" Clyde asks.

"Now what's that supposed to mean?" John asks.

"Cool it, John! We owe you an apology."

"An apology?" Sly, asks.

"Yes! We all acted selfish, high strung, arrogant."

"Self-centered!" Deke, says.

"Overbearing!" James replies.

"Stupid!" Deke, says.

"Idiotic!"

"Cruel!"

"Cold hearted!"

"Pompous ass!"

"Exactly! Connie, I owe you and your sister a very big apology for the way I treated yall. I shouldn't have done what I've done to yall. I know you won't forgive me, so I won't ask. I can't blame you if you don't, because I have acted very sexist."

"Pushy!" Deke replies.

"Conceited!" James says.

"Cold!" Deke replies.

"Heartless!"

"Thoughtless!"

"Sexual!"

"Contact!"

"Gutless!"

"Snake!"

"Exactly! I was hoping we could all be friends."

"You kidding?" Clyde asks.

"No!"

"Fellas, I think we can be friends with, Pazzaz."

"Connie, you serious?" Clyde asks.

"Yes! we all shouldn't be fighting each other anyway. We all need to stick together since there's too many of us destroying each other as it is. If we can make peace let's do it. If we can work together, let's do it. We're all striving to achieve the same goal. So, let's do it------together."

"She's right! James, we accept your apology. and we can be friends." Sly, says.

"Good! Well, we'll be leaving. " James, replies.

"So are we. I can't stand jail." Sly, says.

The rest of the group and the girls along with Mr. MacDonald is outside, waiting for, Sly and company to come out. When they came out everyone watched as Pazzaz come out and rode back to the ranch. Back at the ranch, Pazzaz packs up, and gets ready to leave.

"Well, it's that time." Jim says.

"Yeah, we could've had something here, fellas."

"Could've, should've, would've, Johnny." John says.

"Fellas, don't get discouraged."

"Why not, James?" John asks.

"Because all is not lost."

"No?" They, ask.

"All is not ruined."

"No?" They, ask.

"No!"

"You know something we don't?"

"Yes, John I do."

"What?"

"Let's just say, this won't be our last appearance in Tucson."

"Oh, we're not leaving?" Jim, asks,

"Oh yeah, we are leaving. That's not what I meant by our last appearance. Believe me when I tell you fellas. We're leaving, but we'll be back."

Pazzaz boards the bus, and the bus pulls off. The next day The Cromatics get ready for their final performance. Sly, tells, Sonja that the group is gonna do a special song for the girls for thier final performance. The Cromatics make a little change in their lineup. instead of, Deke singing the lead, Sly sings the lead on this song. When the M.C. announces the group, Sly makes a special dedication for this song. The song is titled, 'Song to Sonja'. Sonja was shocked to hear Sly dedicated a song to her. She was more shocked he wrote a song for her, to her, about her. When the group finish everyone applauds with a standing ovation. Sonja clapped so hard she started crying. She rushed backstage to give, Sly a big hug and a kiss. They didn't have too much time to talk, since The Cromatics were leaving the next day. They had to get everything loaded up on the bus. The next day the group said goodbye to the girls and exchange numbers before they left. On their way out, Mr. MacDonald asks the group if they would return next summer. The Cromatics agreed to come back next year in the summer of "68". The Cromatics say their final goodbyes as this wraps up their gig in 1967 at an all-girls ranch in Tucson, Arizona. The Cromatics promise to keep in touch with their new female friends when they get back home to Newark, New Jersey. The Cromatics can say they have enjoyed their summer in Tucson. And they are looking forward to coming back next year.

www.ingramcontent.com/pod-product-compliance
Lightning Source LLC
LaVergne TN
LVHW051216070526
838200LV00063B/4927